# ED and MR ELEPHANT
# The BIG SURPRISE

# LISA STUBBS

PICCADILLY PRESS • LONDON

"Hurry up, Mr Elephant," said Ed, as he toot, toot, tootled his horn. "I've got a BIG surprise for you today."

"Where are we going?" asked Mr Elephant
as he bounced towards Ed.

"You'll just have to wait and see!" said Ed, smiling.

"We'll need plenty of petrol," said Ed.
"And we have to hurry or we'll be late."
"Why?" asked Mr Elephant.
"You'll just have to wait and see," said Ed.

"Are we there yet?" asked Mr Elephant, as they stopped at the railway crossing.
"No, and now we will be late," fussed Ed, watching the train whizz past.
"Where are we going?" asked Mr Elephant impatiently.
"Wait and see!" said Ed.

"Hello, ducks!" cried Mr Elephant.
"Can the ducks come too?" he asked Ed.
"Yes, but they will have to fly," said Ed. "Do hurry along now, everyone will be waiting."
"Where are we going?" quacked the ducks.
"Wait and see," said Ed.

"Wipe my wipers and spin my wheels," said Ed,
as it started to rain. "We'll never get there on time now."
"I can't wait," laughed Mr Elephant. "But *where*
are we going?"
"Wait and see!" said Ed, splashing through the puddles.

"Nee Naa, Nee Naa, Nee Naa," screamed the big
red fire engine behind Ed.
"Are they coming too?" asked Mr Elephant.
"Not just yet," said Ed. "They've got work to do first.
We're off to have some fun!"

"Wheee!" shouted Ed. "Now we can go quickly and we might still arrive on time."
"Pleeeeease tell me where we are going," pleaded Mr Elephant, who was very excited now.
But all Ed would say was . . . "Wait and see!"

"Oh no!" gasped Ed, nearly in tears as they came to a tree which was blocking the road. "Now we're going to be very late. The others will be wondering where we are."

But Mr Elephant had an idea.

They huffed and puffed and pulled and pushed and in the end they moved the tree!

"Teamwork!" shouted Mr Elephant, as they zoomed off.

"Hooray!" everyone cheered. "They've finally arrived!"
"WOW!" exclaimed Mr Elephant. "A fair! It's brilliant,
and all our friends are here as well!"

"That was a BIG surprise," said Mr Elephant, still munching on some candy floss. "Where are we going next?"

"You'll just have to wait and see!" said Ed.